P9-DMF-026

The Magic School Bus

A SCIENCE CHAPTER BOOK

DINOSAUR DETECTIVES

The Magic School Bus
A science CHAPTER BOOK

DINOSAUR DETECTIVES

SCHOLASTIC INC.
New York   Toronto   London   Auckland   Sydney   Mexico City   New Delhi   Hong Kong

Written by Judith Bauer Stamper.

Illustrations by Ted Enik.

Based on *The Magic School Bus* books
written by Joanna Cole and illustrated by Bruce Degen.

If you purchased this book without a cover, you should be aware that this book is stolen property. It was reported as "unsold and destroyed" to the publisher, and neither the author nor the publisher has received any payment for this "stripped book."

No part of this publication may be reproduced in whole or in part, or stored in a retrieval system, or transmitted in any form or by any means, electronic, mechanical, photocopying, recording, or otherwise, without written permission of the publisher. For information regarding permission, write to Scholastic Inc., Attention: Permissions Department, 555 Broadway, New York, NY 10012.

ISBN 0-439-20423-2

Copyright © 2001 by Joanna Cole and Bruce Degen. Published by Scholastic Inc. All rights reserved.

SCHOLASTIC, THE MAGIC SCHOOL BUS, and associated logos are trademarks and/or registered trademarks of Scholastic Inc.

12 11 10 9 8 7 6 5 4 3   01 02 03 04 05

Designed by Peter Koblish

Printed in the U.S.A.   40

First Scholastic printing, February 2001

The author would like to thank

Dr. Thomas Holtz Jr. for all of his

expert advice in reviewing this manuscript.

 INTRODUCTION

Hi, my name is Ralphie. I am one of the kids in Ms. Frizzle's class.

Maybe you've heard of Ms. Frizzle. (Sometimes we just call her the Friz.) She is a terrific teacher — but a little weird. Things can get really strange in her science class.

She takes us for lots of field trips in the Magic School Bus. Believe me, it's not called *magic* for nothing! We never know what's going to happen when we get on that bus.

Ms. Frizzle likes to surprise us, but we can usually tell when she is planning a special trip — we just look at what she is wearing.

One day, Ms. Frizzle showed up for class in a dress with dinosaurs all over it. She had a special surprise field trip planned. But even the Friz was surprised at where — and when — our field trip took us! Let me tell you all about it.

CHAPTER 1

We were walking down the hallway toward Ms. Frizzle's classroom on a Monday morning. I was really excited to get to school. We had just started a unit on dinosaurs. And I had a big surprise for everyone.

"Do you smell something strange?" Dorothy Ann said, wrinkling up her nose.

"That smell isn't strange," I said. "It's disgusting! EWWW!"

Just then, Ms. Frizzle came rushing out of the classroom. She was wearing a cool dinosaur dress. And she was carrying Wanda's project on dinosaur eggs.

"Clear the hallway!" Ms. Frizzle shouted.

1

"I'm coming through!" Her voice sounded funny because she was pinching her nose shut with one hand. "I've got to get these eggs outside."

Dinosaurs Laid Eggs
by Wanda

Baby dinosaurs hatched from eggs. Dinosaur eggs held the baby animal and a yolk. The yolk was the animal's food until it hatched.

Big plant eaters laid the biggest eggs. Sauropods were heavy, long-necked plant eaters, and they laid football-shaped eggs. Their eggs were 1 foot long and 10 inches wide!

"Yuk! That's rotten egg we smell," Carlos said.

"Technically, it's hydrogen sulfide," Dorothy Ann corrected him.

"Whatever it is," Carlos said, "it's *egg*stremely gross!"

I laughed at Carlos's joke. Everyone else groaned.

As soon as we went into the classroom, we rushed to open the windows. We saw Ms. Frizzle outside dumping the eggs into a garbage bin.

I noticed that Liz was lying on Ms. Frizzle's desk, looking more green than usual. I carried her to the window to get some fresh air. By the time Ms. Frizzle came back, we could all breathe again!

"Those weren't real dinosaur eggs, were they?" Phoebe asked.

"No way!" Dorothy Ann exclaimed. "Dinosaurs are extinct. They died out millions of years ago."

"Did you say dinosaurs stink?" Carlos asked. Everyone groaned again.

"No, Carlos," Dorothy Ann answered.

"They're *extinct*. That means not one member of their species is still alive."

Extinct Is Forever
                    by Dorothy Ann

Dinosaurs are extinct. Not one of their kind is still alive. Dinosaurs became extinct about 65 million years ago. When humans appeared on Earth, dinosaurs had already been dead for millions of years. But dinosaurs were on Earth 1,500 times longer than humans have been so far.

"Class, if there are no dinosaurs around, how do we know they existed?" Ms. Frizzle asked. She was just checking to see if we remembered what we had learned last week.

About twenty hands shot up, including

mine. I was dying to answer the question. I had proof in my backpack. But Ms. Frizzle picked Keesha to answer her question.

"Fossils," Keesha said. "That's how we know about dinosaurs."

"Fantastic, Keesha," Ms. Frizzle said.

"Ms. Frizzle, Ms. Frizzle," I said, waving my hand in the air. "*Please* call on me."

"All right, Ralphie," the Friz said. "What do you have to add?"

I stood up, picked up my backpack, and walked to the front of the room. I reached into my bag and pulled out my surprise. "It's a dinosaur fossil!"

How Fossils Form

by Tim

A fossil is created when an animal or plant dies and is buried in the ground. Over time, the hard parts of the animal, such as bones and teeth, are preserved by surrounding minerals. These hard parts turn into rock and become a fossil.

Fantastic Fossils
by Keesha

We know about dinosaurs through their fossils. A fossil is anything left from a prehistoric animal or plant. There are five main kinds of dinosaur fossils:

- Bones
- Teeth
- Footprints
- Eggs and Nests
- Skin Prints

Fossils give us clues about how dinosaurs looked and how they lived.

"Wow!" Dorothy Ann said. She rushed up to check out my fossil. The rest of the kids followed after her.

"Did that come from a cereal box, Ralphie?" Dorothy Ann said suspiciously. I ignored D.A. For once, I knew something she didn't.

"It certainly looks like a fossil, Ralphie," Ms. Frizzle said. "Where did you get it?"

"I went to visit my grandmother this weekend," I explained. "When I told her about our dinosaur project, she said she had an uncle who hunted dinosaur fossils — way back in 1915. And an old trunk of his was still up in the attic."

"Cool!" Tim said.

"My dad and I went up to the attic and found the trunk," I continued. "Inside there were some picks and maps. And at the bottom of the trunk we found this." I stopped and picked up the fossil.

"Do you know where your uncle found it?" the Friz asked.

"Grandma said he searched for dinosaurs out in the state of Wyoming," I said.

"You mean there were dinosaurs in the United States?" Carlos asked.

"You bet," Ms. Frizzle answered. "Thousands of dino skeletons have been found in the West."

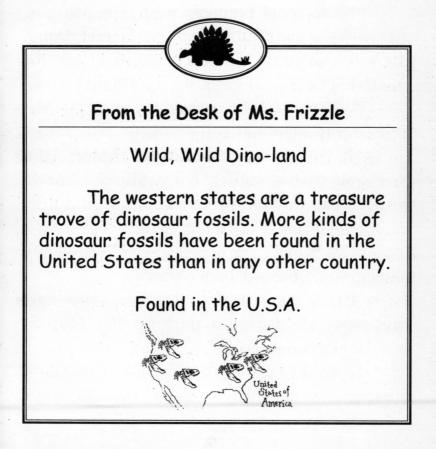

From the Desk of Ms. Frizzle

Wild, Wild Dino-land

The western states are a treasure trove of dinosaur fossils. More kinds of dinosaur fossils have been found in the United States than in any other country.

Found in the U.S.A.

United States of America

"What part of a dinosaur is it?" Phoebe asked, staring at my fossil.

"I think it's a tooth," I said.

"Maybe it's from a *T. rex*," Carlos said.

"I know just the person who can identify this," Ms. Frizzle said. She whipped out her cell phone and punched in a number.

"Hello, can I speak with Dr. Marcus, please?" she said into the phone. "Hello, Doug. It's Valerie Frizzle. Could I bring in a fossil for you to look at? . . . Great, we'll be right there."

"Where are we going?" I asked as Ms. Frizzle put away her cell phone.

"To the Museum of Natural History," the Friz said with a smile. "If Dr. Marcus knows which dinosaur that tooth belongs to, Ralphie, maybe he'll put it in the museum!"

"Oh, wow!" Dorothy Ann yelled. "They have great dinosaur bones there."

"Bring your fossil, Ralphie," the Friz said as we all started to pack up. "Dr. Marcus is a dinosaur detective."

It would be so cool if my fossil was in a museum. I carefully tucked the dinosaur tooth into my backpack. Liz took a flying leap into Ms. Frizzle's schoolbag. She had been acting excited ever since we started studying dinosaurs.

We all headed out of the classroom to the Magic School Bus.

"I wish we could see some real dinosaurs," Keesha said as we piled inside.

"That's impossible!" Dorothy Ann said.

But D.A. forgot one thing. *Nothing* is impossible with the Magic School Bus!

CHAPTER 3

Carlos and Phoebe grabbed my favorite seat — right behind Ms. Frizzle — before I got the chance.

"Sit with me, Ralphie," D.A. asked, patting the seat beside her. It was right behind Carlos and Phoebe.

I knew D.A. just wanted to see my dinosaur fossil, but I sat down anyway.

"So, Dorothy Ann," Carlos said, turning around in his seat. "Why did the dinosaur cross the road?"

"I don't know. To get to the other side?" D.A. guessed.

"No, because the chicken hadn't evolved yet!"

Carlos laughed till tears came to his eyes. D.A. didn't even crack a smile.

"Let me see your dinosaur fossil, Ralphie," D.A. said. "I promise I'll be really, really careful."

"Oh, okay," I agreed, pulling the fossil from my backpack. I cautiously placed it in D.A.'s hand.

Just then, Ms. Frizzle called back to Phoebe and Carlos. "Kids, check the map on my laptop. I want to take the shortest route to the museum."

Carlos grabbed the Friz's laptop and popped it open.

"What keyword should I type in?" he asked. Ms. Frizzle didn't answer. She was busy keeping her eyes on the road.

I leaned forward and looked at the laptop. "Try 'dinosaur,'" I suggested.

Carlos typed in "dinosaur." A second later, a time line popped up on the screen.

Age of Dinosaurs

Dinosaurs ruled the earth during the Mesozoic Era. The Mesozoic Era is divided into three periods.

Mesozoic Era

Triassic Period
251 million yearsago

Plateosaurus
Coelophysis

Jurassic Period
200 million years ago

Brachiosaurus
Allosaurus

Cretaceous Period
144 million years ago

Tyrannosaurus rex
Triceratops

"Now what?" Carlos asked me.

"Try clicking on Triassic," I said. "That dinosaur named *Coelophysis* looks really cool."

Carlos clicked the mouse on Triassic. But the next screen that popped up was really strange. It didn't say anything about the *Coelophysis* or the museum. It just had a lot of icons on it. The only one I recognized was the Magic School Bus. And even it looked strange.

"I wonder what this does?" Carlos asked as he aimed the cursor at the Magic School Bus icon.

"I don't know," I said. "Try it."

Carlos clicked on the Magic School Bus icon. Then something even stranger happened. Two bright signs began to flash on the screen.

One said ESCAPE.

The other said T-TRAVEL.

I was getting a bad feeling about this. I saw Carlos move the cursor to T-Travel. I tried to stop his trigger finger. But he clicked the mouse just as I opened my mouth to scream, "Stop!"

W-H-O-O-S-H!

The sound around us was louder than a jet! Outside the windows, everything turned into a blur. Ms. Frizzle whirled around to stare at Carlos and her laptop.

"No!" she yelled. (She had to yell above the noise.) "You didn't click on T-Travel, did you?"

"Did I do something wrong?" Carlos asked.

For a moment, the Friz's face turned as red as her hair. Then she smiled, and I noticed that familiar twinkle in her eye.

"Hold on tight, everybody!" she shouted. "We're traveling back in T-I-M-E!"

Her words were lost in a weird echo as we left the twenty-first century behind.

We must have traveled millions and millions of years back in time. The centuries were

just flying by outside the windows. Then, all of a sudden, we came to a stop. A dead stop!

It looked like the bus had landed right in the middle of a dinosaur graveyard!

Everybody peered out the windows. We were surrounded by gigantic bones!

CHAPTER 3

"Ms. Frizzle," Keesha cried. "Are we extinct?"

Ms. Frizzle straightened her dinosaur dress and drew a deep breath. "Of course we're not extinct, Keesha," the Friz said. "We're just parked near the rib cage of what looks like a *Plateosaurus*."

"That must mean we're in the Triassic Period," Tim said. "The earliest period of the Mesozoic Era."

"That's the button you told me to push, remember, Ralphie?" Carlos said.

"Uh, yeah," I said, not wanting to look too responsible for this field trip — just in case we never got back to the twenty-first century!

"Well, since we're back in time 225 million years," the Friz said, "we might as well look around. Follow me, class. We're going on a Triassic field trip."

The Friz opened the bus door and slid down a rib bone to the ground. We all slid down after her. We picked our way through the dinosaur skeletons until we got to a dinosaur's skull.

Dino Data File

PLATEO SAURUS
PLAT-ee-oh-SAW-rus

A Plateosaurus was one of the first long–necked plant eaters in the Triassic Period. It stood 27 feet long and weighed 1,500 pounds. It could also rear up and use its hands to pull leaves off trees. **Fun Fact:** *Plateosaurus* had weak teeth. These weren't much help against large predators. Its large thumb claw was its best defense!

"Wow!" said Carlos. "Look at those teeth!"

"Hey, Ralphie," D.A. said, "get out your fossil. Let's see if it matches."

Ms. Frizzle brightened. "That's right, Ralphie, you can be a dinosaur detective, too!"

I pulled the fossil out of my backpack and held it up beside the jawbone of the *Plateosaurus*. The teeth were both flat, but not in the same way.

"Your fossil isn't a *Plateosaurus* tooth," Ms. Frizzle said. "But it is a tooth from a plant eater. You can tell by its shape."

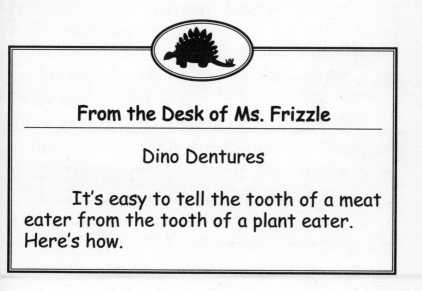

From the Desk of Ms. Frizzle

Dino Dentures

It's easy to tell the tooth of a meat eater from the tooth of a plant eater. Here's how.

Meat eaters all had sharp, pointy teeth.

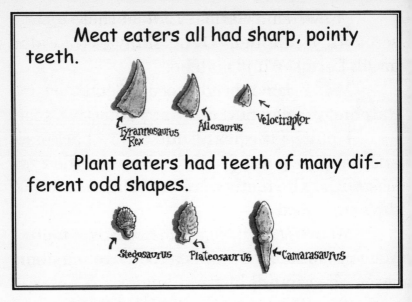

Tyrannosaurus Rex

Allosaurus

Velociraptor

Plant eaters had teeth of many different odd shapes.

Stegosaurus

Plateosaurus

Camarasaurus

"Whew! Check out the fangs on that meat eater. Am I ever glad we're looking for a plant eater," I said.

"But what if a meat eater is looking for us?" Phoebe asked with a quaver in her voice.

"Well, they wouldn't be looking for us on purpose," Dorothy Ann said. "Humans didn't exist at the same time as the dinosaurs."

"Still," Ms. Frizzle said as she picked Liz up off the ground. "Let's just be careful not to call attention to ourselves."

Just then, Wanda let out a bloodcurdling scream. "Yikes! Something slimy just landed on my head!" Wanda yelled.

"So much for not calling attention to ourselves," Tim said under his breath.

We all got quiet thinking about what kind of slimy stuff might have landed on Wanda. Then we heard something weird that gave us a good clue.

MUNCH. CRUNCH. SMACK. It sounded like our lunchroom when everyone was eating. Only a hundred times louder!

"Ms. Frizzle," I said. "I think we have company."

We all looked up at the tops of the trees that surrounded the dinosaur graveyard. We saw a small head with a long snout that was attached to a very long neck.

"Why, it's a real, live *Plateosaurus!*" Ms. Frizzle cried. "Just like the skeletons, only with meat on its bones!"

"Looks like about fifteen hundred pounds of meat to me," Carlos said.

Just then, the *Plateosaurus* drooled some of its food again. It splattered right on my cap.

"EWWW!" I yelled.

"*Plateosaurus* was one of the first dinosaurs to eat plants," the Friz told us. "Triassic jungles were full of tasty treats."

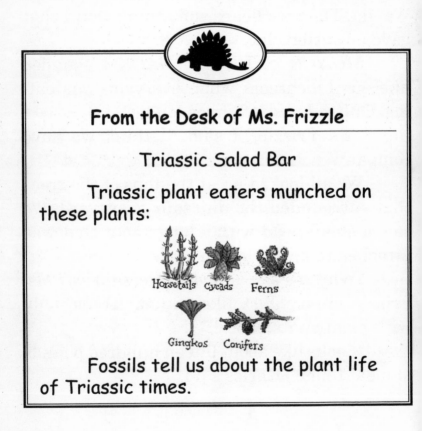

From the Desk of Ms. Frizzle

Triassic Salad Bar

Triassic plant eaters munched on these plants:

Horsetails Cycads Ferns

Gingkos Conifers

Fossils tell us about the plant life of Triassic times.

"Uh-oh," Dorothy Ann said. She pointed to the rest of the tall trees that stood around the skeleton graveyard. There were eight more *Plateosaurus* heads poking out above the treetops. We were surrounded! And, worse yet, dinosaur drool started to fall on us like rain.

"Hey, these guys may be vegetarians," I said, "but they are nasty eaters."

"And they could squash us," Phoebe added.

"Good point, Phoebe," the Friz said, waving us back to the bus. "I think we'll zoom out of here and check out the Triassic world from the air."

We piled inside the bus. The Friz told us to buckle up. Then she pulled down a switch on the Magic School Bus dashboard. There was a rumbling and shaking as the bus turned into the Magic School Bus-copter. Within minutes we were zooming straight up out of the dinosaur graveyard, but it might not have been soon enough.

A *Plateosaurus* tried to take a mouthful of our copter as we passed by, but Ms. Frizzle turned the wheel of the copter just in time and we zoomed into the sky.

CHAPTER 4

"Look down, class," Ms. Frizzle said, piloting us high over the jungle. "You can see what the world looked like two hundred and twenty million years ago."

"It reminds me of my trip to Hawaii," Phoebe said.

"You're right, Phoebe," the Friz said. "Parts of the world in the Triassic Period were like a tropical jungle like Hawaii. But other parts were like deserts."

"Are we flying over Hawaii right now?" Carlos asked.

"No, we're flying over Pangaea," the Friz

answered. "The whole world was one giant continent in Triassic times. Today we call it Pangaea."

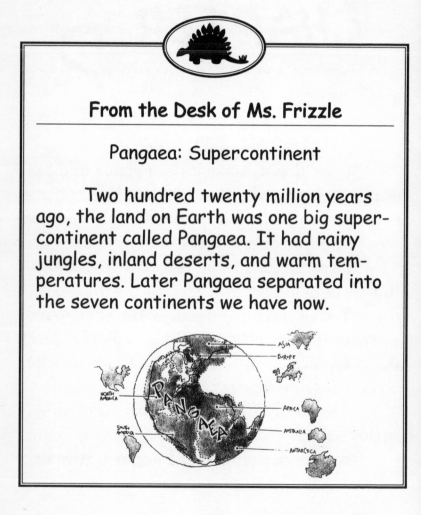

From the Desk of Ms. Frizzle

Pangaea: Supercontinent

Two hundred twenty million years ago, the land on Earth was one big super-continent called Pangaea. It had rainy jungles, inland deserts, and warm temperatures. Later Pangaea separated into the seven continents we have now.

We flew on until the landscape below us changed. It went from the green jungle to a dry desert with only a few plants growing out of the reddish-brown earth.

Below us, I spied some strange animals running down a dry riverbed.

"Ms. Frizzle, Ms. Frizzle," I yelled. "Look down there!"

The Friz and everyone else on board looked down out of the windows. They spotted the pack of yellow-and-green-striped dinosaurs below us.

"They look like giant lizards," Tim said.

At the sound of "lizards," Liz poked her head out of Ms. Frizzle's schoolbag.

"Giant, scary lizards," Wanda added.

"Let's go down for a closer look," the Friz said, bringing the helicopter down for a landing.

"Are you sure this is a good idea?" Phoebe asked.

"Don't worry, Phoebe," the Friz said. "The *Coelophysis* is a meat eater. But it only eats small animals."

Dinosaur Data File

Coelophysis was a fast-moving, thin meat eater. It stood 22 inches high and weighed 40 pounds. These animals hunted in packs.
Fun Fact: The remains of a baby *Coelophysis* have been found in the stomach of an adult *Coelophysis* skeleton. The adult ate its

COELOPHYSIS
SEEL-oh-FY-sis

"Sometimes it eats really small animals," Dorothy Ann added, looking in her field guide. "The *Coelophysis* even eats its own young when it's hungry enough."

"Gross!" Keesha said.

"Cool," Carlos added.

"I want to see these guys in person," Carlos said. "Let's go."

Carlos led us out of the helicopter and down into the riverbed. We could see the tracks of the *Coelophysis* in the damp ground.

"Someday," Ms. Frizzle pointed out, "those tracks will become fossils. And scientists will use them to learn about the *Coelophysis*."

"Ms. Frizzle," Dorothy Ann called out. "Watch out for Liz. I think she's trying to get out of your bag."

But Dorothy Ann's warning came too late. Just as the Friz turned her head to look into her bag, Liz jumped out. She scampered away down the riverbank. Right in the direction that the *Coelophysis* had taken!

"Oh, no!" Wanda said. "Why is Liz running away?"

"I have a feeling she's gone off to meet her ancient cousins," Ms. Frizzle said.

"What if she gets lost in Triassic times forever?" Wanda asked.

"There's no time to find out!" Ms. Frizzle shouted.

We all took off running down the riverbed after Liz. Everyone was looking for our favorite green lizard.

"Wait a minute," I said. "Isn't that Liz

over there?" I pointed to a pile of rocks near a bend in the river.

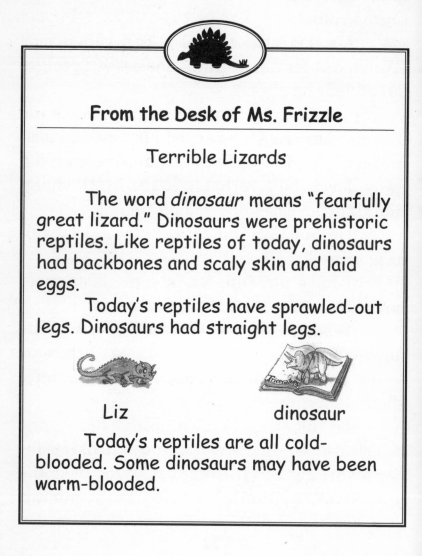

From the Desk of Ms. Frizzle

Terrible Lizards

The word *dinosaur* means "fearfully great lizard." Dinosaurs were prehistoric reptiles. Like reptiles of today, dinosaurs had backbones and scaly skin and laid eggs.

Today's reptiles have sprawled-out legs. Dinosaurs had straight legs.

Liz   dinosaur

Today's reptiles are all cold-blooded. Some dinosaurs may have been warm-blooded.

"Ralphie," Ms. Frizzle whispered. "You're right! See if you can sneak up on her and grab her."

I started to protest. I wasn't sure I could make a sneak attack on Liz. But I knew the Friz was counting on me. I headed off for the rock pile.

Liz was sitting perfectly still, warming herself in the sun. I tiptoed up behind her. But just as I reached out to grab her, she made a flying leap and disappeared around the bend in the riverbed.

I jumped after her. But it wasn't Liz I saw around the bend. Oh, no!

I was looking down into the beady yellow eyes of a *Coelophysis*!

I was so scared that I couldn't move. The dinosaur was little — for a dinosaur. It came to the middle of my chest. And it was skinny. But I didn't like the look in its eyes.

"Ms. Frizzle," I yelled. "Help!"

Luckily for me, Liz came to the rescue. She came running — and ran right over the dinosaur's spiky feet. It shifted its eyes to Liz.

Then it opened its mouth and showed two rows of spiky teeth!

"Liz," I screamed. "Watch out!"

The dinosaur darted its mouth down to gobble up Liz. Just in time, Liz made a flying leap off the ground. There was only one problem. She landed on my shoulder!

I had heard that dinosaurs had small brains. And I was hoping this one was on the stupid side. But I was wrong. The dino jerked its head up to find Liz. Its little yellow eyes lit up with excitement. Food!

Just then, I felt two hands grab hold of me. It was the Friz, to the rescue! She pulled me — and Liz — away from the *Coelophysis*.

"Go away!" the Friz said to the dinosaur, flapping her hands. "Shoo!"

The little dinosaur stopped for a minute and looked hard at the Friz's red hair. Then it made a weird screeching noise. The Friz tucked Liz into her bag and zipped it shut. Then she took my hand and started to run.

"Back to the bus-copter, class!" she

yelled. "Before that guy's friends come."

We all took off running back to the Magic School Helicopter. I glanced back behind us. That was a mistake! I saw the pack of *Coelophysis* coming after us. Their legs were speeding along the ground. And their mouths were open, showing jaws full of sharp teeth.

I suddenly became as fast as an Olympic athlete. I was the first one in the helicopter. Everybody piled in after me. The Friz was last on board. She pulled the hatch closed just as the lead *Coelophysis* reached us. It lifted one clawed hand and left a long scratch on the hatch, right next to the window.

The Friz lost no time taking off. Below us we saw the pack of *Coelophysis* circling the spot where we had been.

"I think we've seen enough of the Triassic Period," I said, wiping the sweat from my forehead.

"Me, too," Ms. Frizzle agreed. "Carlos, get out my laptop. It's time to travel forward in time. We have to track down the owner of that tooth. We're headed for the Jurassic Period."

"What are Jurassic dinosaurs like?" Wanda asked.

"Bigger," Dorothy Ann answered. "Much bigger!"

CHAPTER 5

Outside the window there was a dark swirl of air. The bus-copter turned back into the Magic School Jet. We got to Jurassic times faster than you could say *Pachyrhinosaurus* (that's a big-nosed dinosaur).

When the bus-jet came to a stop, we all jumped up to look out the windows. We had no idea what we would see outside.

"Hey, check this out!" Keesha yelled. "I see two white things. They look like eggs."

Ms. Frizzle poked her head out of Keesha's window. "Wow!" she said. "We've landed beside a nest of dinosaur eggs."

"Do you think we'll see some baby dinosaurs?" Wanda asked. Just then, she got her answer. There was a cracking noise from the nest.

We all piled out of the bus-jet to watch. A little claw poked up out of one of the eggshells. Next came a green head. Finally, the baby dinosaur cracked open the shell and wiggled out. It stood up and took a few wobbly steps.

"Look, more of them are hatching!" D.A. said. "According to my field guide, those look like baby *Diplodocus* dinosaurs."

Dino Data File

The *Diplodocus* was a big plant eater of the Jurassic Period. It measured 90 feet long with a 26-foot neck and a 45-foot tail and it had a small head — only 2 feet long!

Fun Fact: *Diplodocus* swallowed stones to help digest its food. The stones (gastroliths) stayed in its stomach and ground up food.

DIPLODOCUS
dip-LOD-oh-kus

While we watched, ten baby *Diplodocus* hatched around us. Within minutes, they were shaking off their shells and trying out their legs.

The Friz let an excited Liz have a peek at the newly hatched babies.

All of a sudden, I had a scary thought.

"What if their mother comes back?" I asked the Friz. "Will she get mad at us for being near her babies?"

"Hmm, that's a good point, Ralphie. The mother is probably not *too* far away!" Ms. Frizzle answered. The babies started to scramble out of their shells. "Look!" Ms. Frizzle pointed. "The babies need to find a hiding place before a predator finds them."

We followed behind the baby *Diplodocus* as they scurried off into the woods. Not far from the nest we came across another skeleton. The Friz said it was the skeleton of an adult *Diplodocus.*

I pulled my fossil tooth out of my backpack and held it up against the *Diplodocus* tooth. Everyone else stopped to look, too. No

match yet. Being a dinosaur detective took a lot of work!

"Phoebe, wait for us!" Ms. Frizzle yelled. We saw Phoebe heading into the Jurassic forest behind the babies. I think she had fallen in love with them.

We ran after Phoebe, but by the time we got into the forest, she had disappeared. We all scattered, trying to find her. I ran from tree to tree calling her name. After a while, I got so tired that I sat down against a big tree trunk.

A minute later, the tree trunk moved. Then I noticed that the tree trunk had toenails. Really big toenails!

"Ms. Frizzle!" I screamed.

The Friz came running up. "Oh my, Ralphie, you've found a *Brachiosaurus*!"

"Does that mean 'giant dinosaur,' by any chance?" I asked, looking fifty feet up into the sky at the dinosaur's head.

"No, its name means 'arm lizard,'" the Friz explained. "But it's one of the biggest dinosaurs that ever lived!"

I tried to look up into its mouth to see if

Dino Data File

The *Brachiosaurus* was one of the biggest of the Jurassic giants. It grew to 50 feet tall, 85 feet long, and up to 80 tons. It had no predators and spent most of its time eating.
Fun Fact: *Brachiosaurus* needed a huge heart to pump blood to its faraway brain. There is speculation that it had a problem with blood pressure!

my tooth was a match but the mouth was too high up.

The other kids joined us in the shade of the *Brachiosaurus*'s leg. We watched as the huge dinosaur worked its jaws back and forth.

"Do you think it's eaten Phoebe?" Keesha asked.

"Not to worry, Keesha!" Ms. Frizzle said. "The *Brachiosaurus* is a plant eater. It's not interested in eating an animal like Phoebe."

From the Desk of Ms. Frizzle

Dino Diets

Dinosaurs were carnivores (meat eaters) and herbivores (plant eaters). There was a higher number of herbivores than carnivores.

Some plant eaters had long necks to reach the tops of trees and had large stomachs to digest plant fibers. Meat eaters had strong legs and sharp teeth to hunt down and kill their prey.

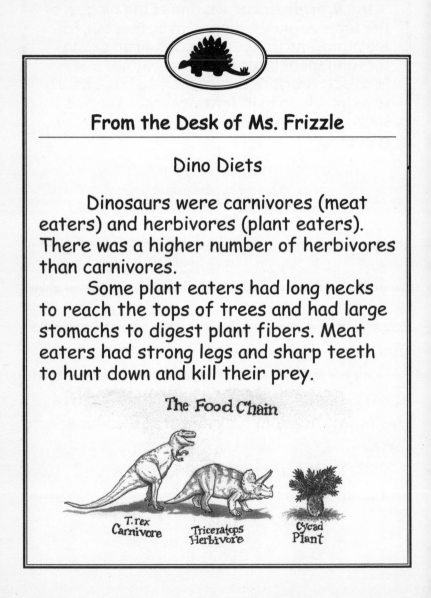

The Food Chain

T. rex
Carnivore

Triceratops
Herbivore

Cycad
Plant

"Hey, Carlos," I said. "How do you know if there's a dinosaur in your refrigerator?"

"How?" Carlos asked.

"You look for footprints in the pizza!"

Carlos and I doubled over laughing. Everyone else groaned.

Just then, the *Brachiosaurus* took a few steps toward us to eat another tree.

"Get out of the way!" Ms. Frizzle yelled. We all scurried backward.

"What if it sees us?" Tim asked. "Would it try to kill us?"

Dinosaur Brainpower

Scientists can tell how smart a dinosaur was by its EQ. EQ stands for Encephalization Quotient. EQ compares the size of a dinosaur's brain to that of its body. Scientists believe dinosaurs were not very bright.

The dumbest dinosaurs were big plant eaters like *Brachiosaurus* and *Apatosaurus.*

The smartest dinosaurs were smaller meat eaters like *Velociraptor.*

Ms. Frizzle shook her head. "Not on purpose, Tim," she said. "This dinosaur is a plant eater and very peaceful."

Suddenly, the huge dinosaur took steps in our direction. It might be peaceful. But that much dinosaur could still be dangerous!

We all ran. Ahead, I saw the opening of a cave.

"Come on," I yelled back to everybody. "We'll be safe inside."

We all sprinted into the cave. But we weren't alone in there. And we definitely weren't safe!

CHAPTER 6

My scream echoed off the walls of the cave. It sounded like a horror movie. And the dinosaur that came from the back of the cave was a nightmare come true!

It was over fifteen feet tall and thirty feet long. It moved toward me on two powerful legs. Its arms were short, but there were sharp claws at the end of its three-fingered hands.

But its mouth was what really caught my eye. Its big jaws were filled with long, jagged teeth. And it seemed to smile when it saw me.

"Run, Ralphie!" I heard the Friz yell. "That's an *Allosaurus*. It's a carnivore!"

In case you don't remember, a carnivore is a meat eater. I remembered. And I ran!

The *Allosaurus* made a swipe at me with its claws. But I ducked just in time. I saw Ms. Frizzle and the rest of the class running to hide under the roots of a giant tree not far away. I sped through the underbrush to join them.

"That was close, Ralphie," the Friz said as I slid to safety under the tree.

"Too close," I added. "I hope that *Allosaurus* has a low EQ."

"Bad news," the Friz said. "*Allosaurus* is on the smart side, for a dinosaur."

The *Allosaurus* came crashing through the trees, closer to where we were hiding.

"Ms. Frizzle," D.A. said. "Can we go home now?"

"I'm sorry, D.A.," the Friz whispered. "My laptop is back on the bus. And anyway, we can't leave without Phoebe."

Just then, a prehistoric mammal that looked a lot like a mouse crawled over Wanda's foot. She let out another bloodcurdling scream.

I saw the head of the *Allosaurus* stop in midair. It seemed to take a few moments to think about the scream. Then it headed in our direction.

Dino Data File

An *Allosaurus* was the biggest meat eater in North America in Jurassic times. It ate mostly small and medium–sized plant eaters. The *Allosaurus* couldn't break its fall with its small front feet when running, but it could get up again.

Fun Fact: When hunting in a pack, a group of *Allosaurus* could even kill a huge plant eater like a *Diplodocus.*

ALLOSAURUS
AL-oh-SAW-rus

"Sorry!" Wanda whispered.

I looked at Ms. Frizzle. Her red hair seemed to be sticking straight out of her head. She held up a finger for us to be quiet.

The *Allosaurus* stomped closer, then stopped. We heard the sound of more big feet, thundering through the forest. The *Allosaurus* had heard them, too. It reared up higher on its back legs and opened its mouth.

In a few minutes, two *Stegosaurus* came into view. They crashed through the trees, swinging their heavy bodies from side to side.

Dino Data File

The *Stegosaurus* was 9 feet tall and 30 feet long. It had 17 bony plates sticking up out of its back. It used these plates for temperature control, defense, and mating.
Fun Fact: *Stegosaurus* had a flexible tail that ended with 4-foot spikes. The spikes could wound and drive off a predator.

The *Allosaurus* had forgotten all about little old us. Its brain was busy figuring out how to get a *Stegosaurus* steak for dinner.

The carnivore waited until the two *Stegosaurus* were walking close by. Then it attacked! The *Allosaurus* slashed out at the smaller *Stegosaurus* with its sharp claws. It made a deep wound in the side of the young dinosaur.

But the fight wasn't over. The older *Stegosaurus* came around to the side of the *Allosaurus*. Turning its back to the enemy, it whipped out its spiked tail. The *Allosaurus* roared in pain as the spike dug into its flesh.

The battle was short but brutal. The *Allosaurus* attacked the young *Stegosaurus* until it fell dead on the ground. The older *Stegosaurus* was wounded, but it got away. Then the *Allosaurus* fell on its prey and began to devour it.

"Gross!" Wanda said. "I can't watch."

"This is a perfect time for us to escape," the Friz said. "And we still have to find Phoebe."

Dinosaur Defense
by Tim

 With hungry meat eaters all around, plant-eating dinosaurs needed all the protection they could get.
- Triceratops had sharp horns.
- Stegosaurus had tail spikes.
- Plateosaurus had thumb claws.
- Diplodocus and Apatosaurus were really huge.
- Sauropeta was covered with bony plates like armor.
- Ankylosaurus had a club at the end of its tail.
- Hypsilophodon used its speed to escape from predators.

We crept out from under the giant tree roots. Then we headed back to where we had last seen Phoebe.

"Phoebe!" the Friz called out. Her voice echoed through the Jurassic forest.

"Over here!" We heard a familiar voice answer. In a few minutes, we found Phoebe sitting in a grassy clearing. She was playing with the ten baby *Diplodocus*. She looked really happy!

"Can we take them home, Ms. Frizzle?" Phoebe asked. "They'd make great classroom pets."

"Until they got a few months old," Tim said. "By then, they'd be bigger than our classroom!"

"No, Phoebe," the Friz said. "They belong just where they are — in Jurassic times."

"Ms. Frizzle," I interrupted her to ask, "do you smell something burning?"

The Friz stopped to sniff the air. So did everyone else.

"A forest fire!" the Friz shouted. "Look, there's a wall of smoke coming through the trees!"

"Head back to the bus," she ordered. "It's time to say good-bye to Jurassic times."

"But what about the babies?" Phoebe pleaded. "We can't just leave them here."

"You know what? I saw a river when we landed. It was just on the other side of their nest," Carlos said. "Maybe we could carry them to the other side where the fire won't reach them."

"Great idea, Carlos," the Friz said. "But hurry!"

We picked up the *Diplodocus* babies and rar with them toward the Magic School Jet and the river.

Behind us, we could hear the fire crackling through the trees. Other dinosaurs were starting to run from it, too.

Finally we saw the bus-jet and the river. Phoebe carried the first baby across the shallow river. I brought across the last one.

When they were all safe on the other side of the water, we ran for the bus-jet.

"Wow!" I said as I sat down. "These seats are getting hot!"

Ms. Frizzle was busy typing on her keyboard. I looked out the window and saw a wall of flame coming toward us.

Just as things were getting too hot to handle, we all heard a loud *WHOOSH*!

And the Jurassic Period was left behind us in a big blur.

CHAPTER 3

Time was whizzing by outside the windows of the Magic School Jet.

"Where . . . I mean, when . . . are we headed, Ms. Frizzle?" Wanda asked.

"What do you mean *when*?" Arnold asked. "We were almost burnt to a crisp. Don't you think it's time to go home?"

"Just one more stop, Arnold. We're still in search of an owner for Ralphie's tooth. The Cretaceous Period is next!" the Friz answered, clicking on the screen of her laptop.

Dorothy Ann had her head buried in her dinosaur field guide. "Hey, Ralphie," she said. "You have a great chance of finding the owner of your fossil now. There were many more plant eaters in the Cretaceous Period than ever before."

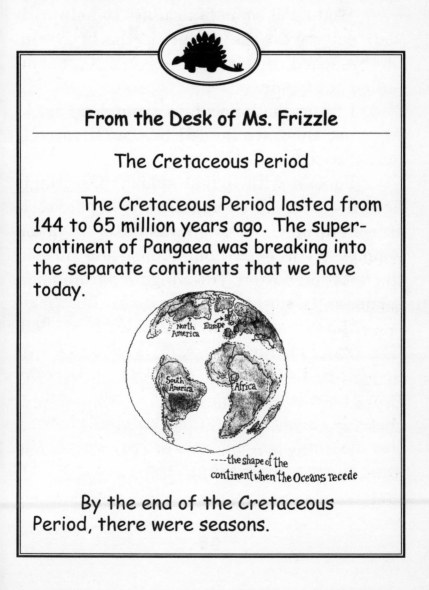

From the Desk of Ms. Frizzle

The Cretaceous Period

The Cretaceous Period lasted from 144 to 65 million years ago. The super-continent of Pangaea was breaking into the separate continents that we have today.

----the shape of the
continent when the Oceans recede

By the end of the Cretaceous Period, there were seasons.

"I don't mind checking out the teeth of dead dinosaurs," I said. "But it's not easy to make a live dinosaur say, 'A-h-h-h.'"

"You need some binoculars to help with your detective work, Ralphie," the Friz said. She reached under the driver's seat and pulled out a pair.

I hung the binoculars around my neck. And just then, we landed in the Cretaceous Period with a splash!

I mean with a real splash. The Magic School Jet crash-landed into a big lake. It started to sink, and there was water up to the windows! The Friz thought fast and pushed the flotation button. The wings separated and turned into four big, floating inner tubes.

"Look over by the shore!" Carlos yelled. "It's a herd of rhinoceroses."

"No, it's a herd of *Triceratops*," Dorothy Ann corrected him.

"Let's get closer," the Friz said, steering the floating bus-jet nearer to where the *Triceratops* were grazing.

Dino Data File

The *Triceratops* looked like a rhinoceros and had three horns on its face and a bony plate (frill) behind its skull. It walked slowly on four short legs and was one of the last horned dinosaurs to exist.

Fun Fact: *Triceratops* had a good defense sys–tem. It charged an enemy with its horned head, just as rhinos do today.

TRICERATOPS
Try-SER-a-tops

I checked out the *Triceratops*'s teeth through my binoculars.

"None of them look like my tooth fossil."

"Why are they called *Triceratops*, Ms. Frizzle?" Tim asked.

"Good question, Tim," the Friz said. "Many dinosaurs were named for the way they looked."

Name That Dino

A dinosaur is named by the scientist who first finds its fossils. Dinos are named for:
• Something special about the way they looked
Triceratops means "roughened three-horned face."
• Something special about the way they lived
Maiasaura means "good mother lizard."
Maiasaura took good care of their babies.
• The place where they were found
Utahraptor was found in the state of Utah.

"Hey, Ralphie," Carlos asked. "What does a *Triceratops* sit on?"

"Tell me, Carlos," I said.

"Its tricera-bottom!"

"Hmmm," Keesha said, trying to ignore us. "Things are so nice and peaceful in the Cretaceous Period."

"Uh-oh, you spoke too soon," Tim said. He pointed to the other side of the lake.

"Troodon!" Dorothy Ann gasped.

Dino Data File

A *Troodon* was named for its "wounding teeth" and was the size of an adult human. It could hold its prey with its three long, clawed fingers.

Fun Fact: *Troodon* was the smartest dinosaur. It had the largest brain in proportion to its body weight.

TROODON
TROE-o-don

The group of *Troodon* were prowling along the water's edge. They weren't much taller than humans. But they had a wicked look in their big eyes.

All of a sudden, the *Troodon* saw the herd of *Triceratops* across the water. Quick as lightning, they sped up on their skinny, fast legs.

"We've got to warn the *Triceratops*! My field guide said that *Troodon* will eat the babies of other dinosaurs!" Dorothy Ann shouted.

I leaned over Ms. Frizzle and honked the bus's horn. Ms. Frizzle stepped on the gas and headed the bus even closer to the herd.

The *Triceratops* looked up and saw the Magic School Bus churning toward them. With loud bellows, the herd took off into the woods.

The *Troodon* were still chasing the herd. But the *Triceratops* had a good head start. They left the *Troodon* in the dust.

"All right!" Carlos said, giving me a high five. "We outsmarted the *Troodon*."

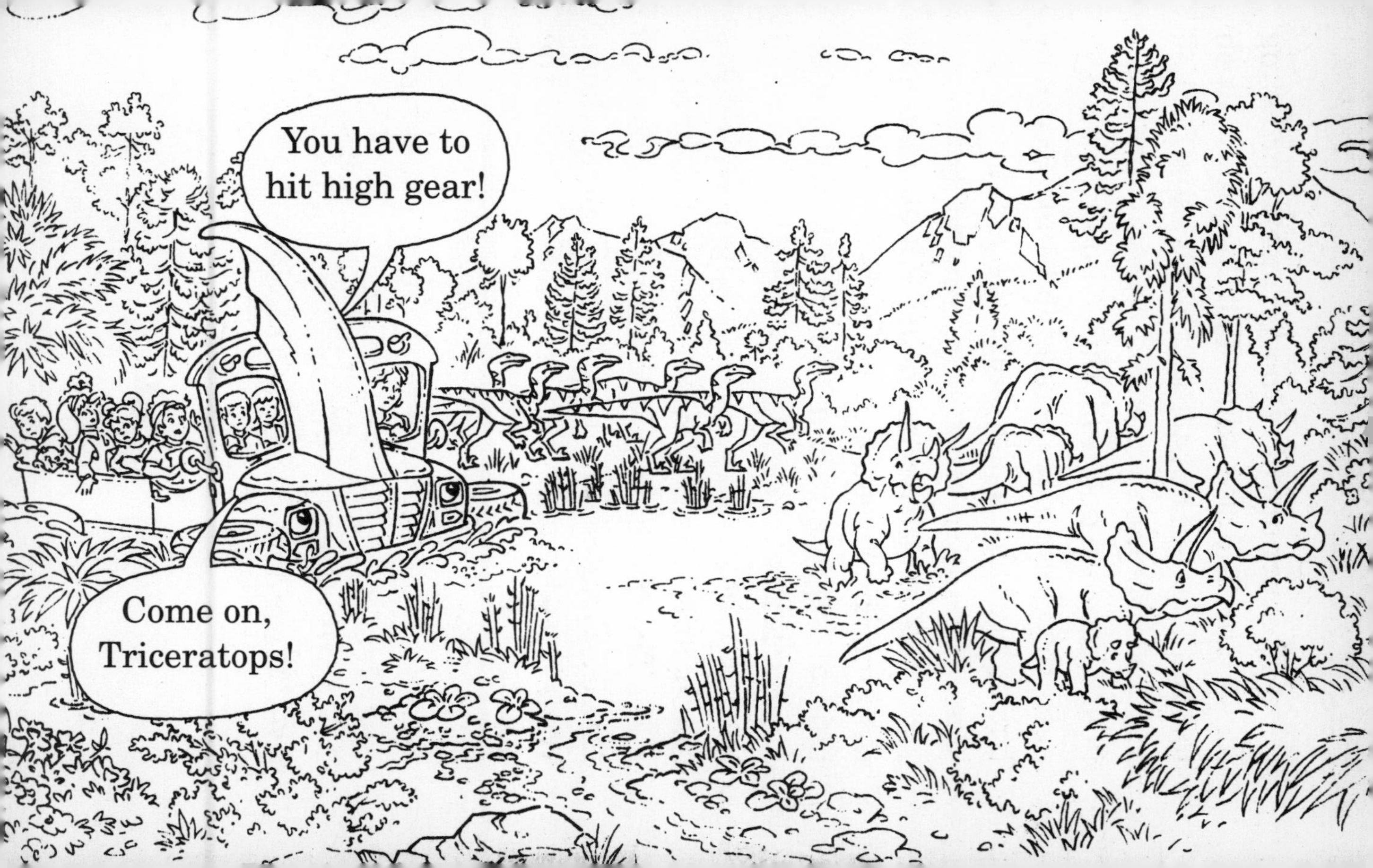
You have to hit high gear!
Come on, Triceratops!

"Come on, kids," the Friz said. "Let's see if we can find the dino with Ralphie's tooth fossil. I'll park the bus up on the shore."

Ms. Frizzle released the air from our float and it turned back into a bus as we drove onto dry land. We scrambled out, ready to track down more dinosaurs.

"This is so much fun!" Wanda said.

But, just then, we heard a loud roar echo through the forest. It was followed by a sharp animal scream. Then the forest was quiet. Dead quiet!

CHAPTER 8

"What was that?" Phoebe asked in a scared whisper.

"I don't know," the Friz answered. "But I can guess."

"Me too," Dorothy Ann said. "I'll bet it was *T. rex*!"

A shiver ran up and down my spine. I pulled out the fossil tooth from my bag. "Let's check out a few more jawbone skeletons," I said, "and then get out of here! I don't want to run into any more live dinosaurs."

Finding skeletons was not a problem. There were plenty of them around. *T. rex* must have been a messy eater — he just left his bones lying around after dinner.

Ms. Frizzle bent down over the jawbone of a medium-sized dinosaur. "Look, class, this was a duckbill dinosaur," she said. "It had hundreds of rows of spiky teeth."

"Those must have been a nightmare to brush!" Keesha said.

"How about this guy?" Tim called out. He was kneeling beside a huge skull.

"That belonged to a domehead dinosaur," Ms. Frizzle explained. "These are both plant eaters, Ralphie. Get our your fossil and see if you have a match."

I studied both jawbones, but neither contained teeth that matched my fossil tooth.

We walked farther on into the woods to find more skeletons. Up ahead, there was a sudden rustling in the trees. We saw a spiky tail with a huge club at the end disappear through the trees in front of us.

"That was an *Ankylosaurus,*" Dorothy Ann said. "I'd recognize that tail anywhere."

Dino Data File

Ankylosaurus was covered by an armor of thick, bony plates. It had a big, bony club at the end of its tail and could break the legs of predators with its tail club.
Fun Fact: *Ankylosaurus*'s whole body was covered with bony plates and spikes. Even its eyelids had bony shutters.

ANKYLOSAURUS
an-KY-loh-SAW-rus

Meanwhile, I had found something exciting on the ground.

"Ms. Frizzle!" I yelled. "Check out these tracks." I felt like a real dino detective. I had spotted some huge footprints on the damp forest floor.

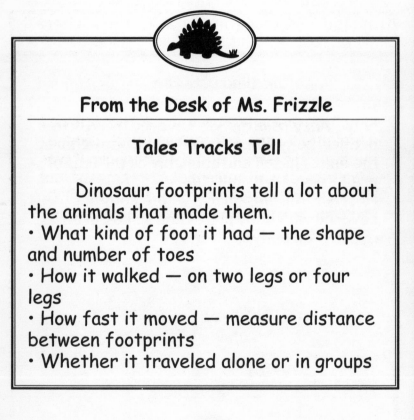

From the Desk of Ms. Frizzle

Tales Tracks Tell

Dinosaur footprints tell a lot about the animals that made them.
• What kind of foot it had — the shape and number of toes
• How it walked — on two legs or four legs
• How fast it moved — measure distance between footprints
• Whether it traveled alone or in groups

Ms. Frizzle took out her ruler and started to measure the prints.

"One and a half feet long," she muttered. "And about twelve feet apart."

"According to my research," Dorothy Ann said, "we're looking at the tracks of a *Tyrannosaurus rex*!"

Dino Data File

A *Tyrannosaurus rex* was named for its personality: Its name means "tyrant lizard king." It grew to 40 feet long, 20 feet tall, and it weighed 7 tons. A *T. rex* had good vision, a keen sense of smell, and a smart brain. It was a fast runner and could make quick turns, but if it fell while running, the impact could kill it. **Fun Fact:** *T. rex* could eat up to 200 pounds of meat and bones in one bite!

TYRANNOSAURUS REX
Tie-RAN-oh-SAW-rus rex

"These tracks certainly are fresh!" Ms. Frizzle said. "The *Tyrannosaurus rex* can't be far away."

"Oh, bad. Oh, bad," Keesha said. "What if the *Ankylosaurus* walks right into it?"

"Maybe we can chase it away in time," D.A. said. She took off after the *Ankylosaurus* before Ms. Frizzle could stop her.

We all hurried after D.A., walking in the tracks of the *T. rex*. The tracks climbed steadily up to the top of a hill. We were huffing and puffing by the time we reached the top. But when we got there, the view was really awesome!

A big grassy plain spread out below us. I couldn't believe how much we could see. In the distance, there was the herd of *Triceratops*. On the other side of the lake was a group of *Troodon*. But one dinosaur stood out among the rest. It looked like a king. In fact, it was one — *Tyrannosaurus rex*.

The *T. rex* stalked back and forth on the plain, looking for prey. It was huge, but it still

moved quickly on its powerful legs. Suddenly, it came to a standstill.

I pulled out my binoculars and took a close look. I almost wished I hadn't! The binoculars zoomed right in on *T. rex*'s head. Its nose was moving up and down with the scent of prey. Its huge jaws were wide open. I saw bone-crunching teeth that were each almost nine inches long. I stopped counting them after I reached fifty!

"Oh, no!" Dorothy Ann said. "There's the *Ankylosaurus,* walking right into *T. rex*'s trap!"

I focused my binoculars back to the edge of the clearing. The *Ankylosaurus* was just coming out of the trees. When it saw the *Tyrannosaurus rex,* it snarled with fear. I zoomed in on its teeth with my binoculars. They were a perfect match. I had an *Ankylosaurus* fossilized tooth in my hand!

But an *Ankylosaurus* tooth is no match for a jawful of *Tyrannosaurus* teeth! The king of the dinosaurs attacked. He was fast and deadly! It was not a pretty sight.

"Ms. Frizzle," Arnold said. "I don't want to be a dino dinner. Can we go back to school now?"

"Ralphie, are you ready?" the Friz asked.

"My detective work is done," I said, tucking my fossil into my backpack.

"Uh, Ms. Frizzle," Carlos said, pointing down to the plain. "Maybe that *Ankylosaurus* was just an appetizer. *T. rex* still looks hungry. And he's heading our way!"

We made some fast tracks ourselves, back to the Magic School Bus. After we all piled inside, the Friz flipped open her laptop. She typed in today's date and then clicked on T-Travel.

WHOOSH! We were on our way back home.

"So, Carlos," I yelled to be heard. "I've got one for you. What do you get when dinosaurs crash their cars?"

"What?" Carlos asked.

"*Tyrannosaurus* wrecks!"

CHAPTER 9

We landed back in the Magic School Bus's special space in the school parking lot.

"Home sweet home!" Wanda yelled. "No meat-eating dinosaurs anywhere!"

As we piled out of the bus, Keesha asked, "Did we really travel back in time, Ms. Frizzle? Or was that just a totally strange dream?"

Ms. Frizzle gave Keesha a mysterious smile. But when I stepped out of the bus, she pulled me aside.

"Look, Ralphie," the Friz said. She pointed to a deep scratch next to the windshield of the bus. "I guess we'll have to replace that window," she added with a wink.

I remembered the *Coelophysis* scratching the hatch way back in the Triassic Period. I met the Friz's eyes and winked back.

When we got into the classroom, Ms. Frizzle's friend from the museum, Dr. Marcus, was waiting for us. He said he'd been worried since we never showed up at the museum.

I pulled out my dinosaur fossil to show him.

"I'll bet you can't guess what this is," he said to me.

"I know what it is," I said. "It's an *Anky-losaurus* tooth."

"Amazing, young man," Dr. Marcus said. "You're absolutely right, and I have just the place for an *Ankylosaurus* tooth at the museum. That is, if you'd like to donate it."

"I'd be happy to," I replied. "I've seen enough dinosaur teeth today to last a lifetime."

Dr. Marcus gave me a funny look, but I just looked at the rest of the class and smiled.

Dr. Marcus stayed at school and answered our questions about dinosaurs. Here are our top ten dinosaur questions. Do you know the answers? Find out on the next pages.

1. Which dinosaur's name means "big-nosed"?

2. What are some examples of dinosaur fossils?

3. Which dinosaur was the biggest?

4. Which dinosaur was the smallest?

5. What was the first dinosaur ever found?

6. Was the Jurassic Period before or after the Triassic?

7. In what country have the most types of dinosaurs been found?

82

8.   What museum has the most di-
     nosaur skeletons?

9.   Which dinosaur had tracks 12 feet
     apart?

10. Where was the largest set of fossil
     footprints ever found?

Answers:

1. *Pachyrhinosaurus*
2. bones, skin prints, tracks, teeth, eggs
3. *Argentinosaurus* from the mid-Cretaceous Period. It weighed 800–1000 tons.
4. *Scipionyx*
5. *Megalosaurus*
6. after
7. United States
8. American Museum of Natural History in New York
9. *T. rex*
10. Wyoming